FURBALL
SPY CAT
He has a licence to CHILL.
ADRIAN BECK

LARRIKIN House

MEET YOUR
FRIENDLY
SPY TEAM!

DOUBLE
OH YEAH!
FURBALL
SPECIAL SKILL
LOOKS
DELUXE
IN A TUX!
FUN
FACT!
Often
sleeps-in till
it's bedtime
again.

SPECIAL SKILL
SHE'S A KARATE CAT!
FUN FACT!
Her happy face IS her angry face.
JADE
SNAP!
SPECIAL SKILL
MAKING SPY GADGETS!
KIT
FUN FACT!
Gets nervous when MISSILES target him.
UH-OH ...
TAP TAP TAP

HI THERE, I'M KIT!

Right now, I'm on a **TOP SECRET MISSION!**

(Trust me, I don't NORMALLY dress up like a banana.)

Let me explain . . . These are my friends, Jade and Furball. We're all **SUPER SPIES**, working for **MEOW-6**. (We fight **BADDIES!**)

Our enemies work for an EVIL organisation, known as KLAWZ!

Fortunately, Furball has taken down more KLAWZ villains than he's had fish tacos. (And that's a LOT!)

As usual, we're in the middle of SAVING THE WORLD!
Evil KLAWZ agents are planning to CRASH A ROCKET INTO THE MOON!
Why would anyone want to do this? WHAT'S WRONG WITH THE MOON?
YOU BEAUT FRUIT
I hear it has NO ATMOSPHERE.

Furball can joke all he likes, but this is **SERIOUS!**

I only hope Jade can bust into the control tower.

Suddenly, my heart starts **RACING** as I look over at the launch pad. UH-OH ...

'Kit to Furball, come in! The rocket is **TAKING OFF!** I've lost sight of you. What's your position?'

'Tell me you brought along some of your **SPY GADGETS**, Kit,' says Jade, as I spot her up in the control tower. 'I think Furball needs a hand.'

'What makes you say that?' I ask.

'WILD GUESS,' Jade replies.

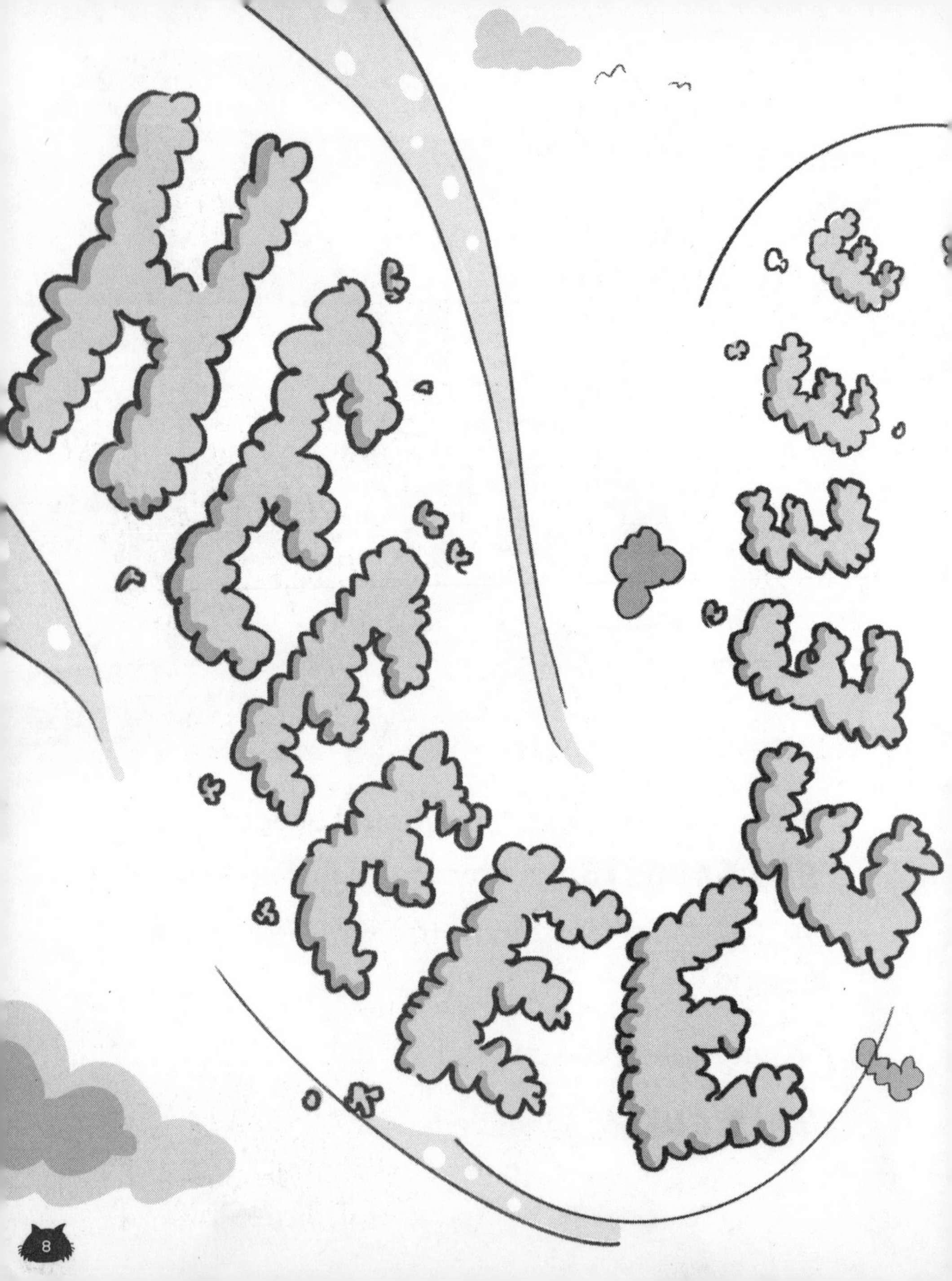

'Furball, the onboard camera shows the rocket is on AUTOPILOT,' says Jade. 'You'll need to climb up to the cockpit and **TAKE CONTROL, ASAP!**'

'Jade! Can you send me a photo of the cockpit controls?' I say. 'I **MIGHT** be able to talk Furball through it.'

'First you'll need to **TALK HIM INTO IT!**' Jade says, as she sends me a pic.

'OOH! THIS MIGHT JUST WORK!'

I say, zooming in on the photo. 'Furball, do you ***SMELL*** anything up there?'

‘Looks like the last astronaut to pilot the rocket left behind their **LUNCH!**’ I explain. ‘I’m guessing it’s . . .’

‘**A TUNA SANDWICH!**’ cries Furball.

I'LL SAVE YOU!

'Is he talking about the ***MOON*** or the ***SANDWICH?***' asks Jade on the walkie-talkie.

'Hopefully both,' I reply. 'Go, Furball!' I cry, glad he doesn't share my FEAR OF HEIGHTS. Besides, at the rate he's moving, Furball clearly has a need . . . ***A NEED FOR FEED!***

'Okay, Furball,' I say, trying to help him work out the rocket's controls. 'The first thing you need to do is . . .'

'EAT!' he interrupts. 'Nom, nom, nom!'

'Furball, if you don't turn the rocket around RIGHT NOW it'll be too late. **THE MOON WILL BE DESTROYED!**' I cry. 'It's a complicated process, buuuut . . .'

'Okay, I just pressed a button with my **BUTT** – good advice, Kit!' says Furball.

'What's the **GOOD NEWS?**' I ask.

'The rocket is returning to the launch site. I'm coming in to land,' says Furball. 'Saved by the **BUTT!**'

'And the **BAD NEWS?**' asks Jade, as I hold my breath.

'I've **FINISHED** my sandwich,' Furball replies.

'Hey, did you ***NOT*** hear the bit about my sandwich?' grumbles Furball.

NOOOOOO!

2

Later, we return home to **MEOW-6** HQ to celebrate yet another successful mission.

'We got away with our mission today, Kit,' says Jade. 'But it was close.'

'Yeah, **TOO CLOSE!**' I reply. 'I've always wanted to say that . . . I've ALSO always wanted to **TAP DANCE**.'

'Hmmm. Maybe I should have brought more **SPY GADGETS** to the mission. That's my job, after all,' I say. 'But I'm not sure my last few inventions have been all that useful . . . I just finished testing a toothbrush that turns into a **SUPER MAGNET!**'

'I also created a **GADGET WATCH** that attracts LIGHTNING!'

'And **UNDERPANTS** that expand into a **PARACHUTE!**'

'Don't **EVER** make me picture that again,' says Jade, angrily. 'Or I'll use my KARATE SKILLS on **YOU!**'

When we're not on missions, Jade is Furball's karate coach. It's **NOT** an easy job. Although she seems to like it.

Just then, our spy boss, **MS BIG WIG**, joins the celebration. She's with **BARROT** her pet **PARROT** who always tries to repeat whatever people say. But he doesn't *always* get it right.

'I have a **SURPRISE** for all your hard work!' says Big Wig. (Which REALLY isn't like her.)

'I don't do surprises,' says Jade. 'Unless it's ME sneaking up on a room full of bad guys! And then I do surprises **REAL GOOD!**'

As Big Wig leaves, I rip open the invitation to find three tickets inside. ***COOL!***

'Guys, have you seen where I put my floaties?'

Because we're going to ***WET WILLY'S WATERWORLD!***

3

There are soooo many things to see and do at **WET WILLY'S WATERWORLD**, I don't know where to start!

'Kit, you know how he feels about his tux,' says Jade. 'Remember last week? He didn't even take it off to **WASH** . . .'

OH MY GOSH!
CAR WASH
WHIIIIR
WHIIIIR
MORE BUBBLES, LESS TROUBLES!

Once we get inside the waterpark, I soon realise I've **NEVER** seen Jade so excited.

'WATERSLIDES RULE!' she cries.

AUUUUUUUUUUGH!
DROP OF DOOM
GULP.

'Umm. I had a **BIG** breakfast. Would it be okay if we start with a nice gentle float in the kiddie pool?' I ask. 'And the line for the **DROP OF DOOM** is sure to be very long . . .'

I quickly run off to get us all a floating tube. The worker from the park seems **VERY KEEN** to hand them out.

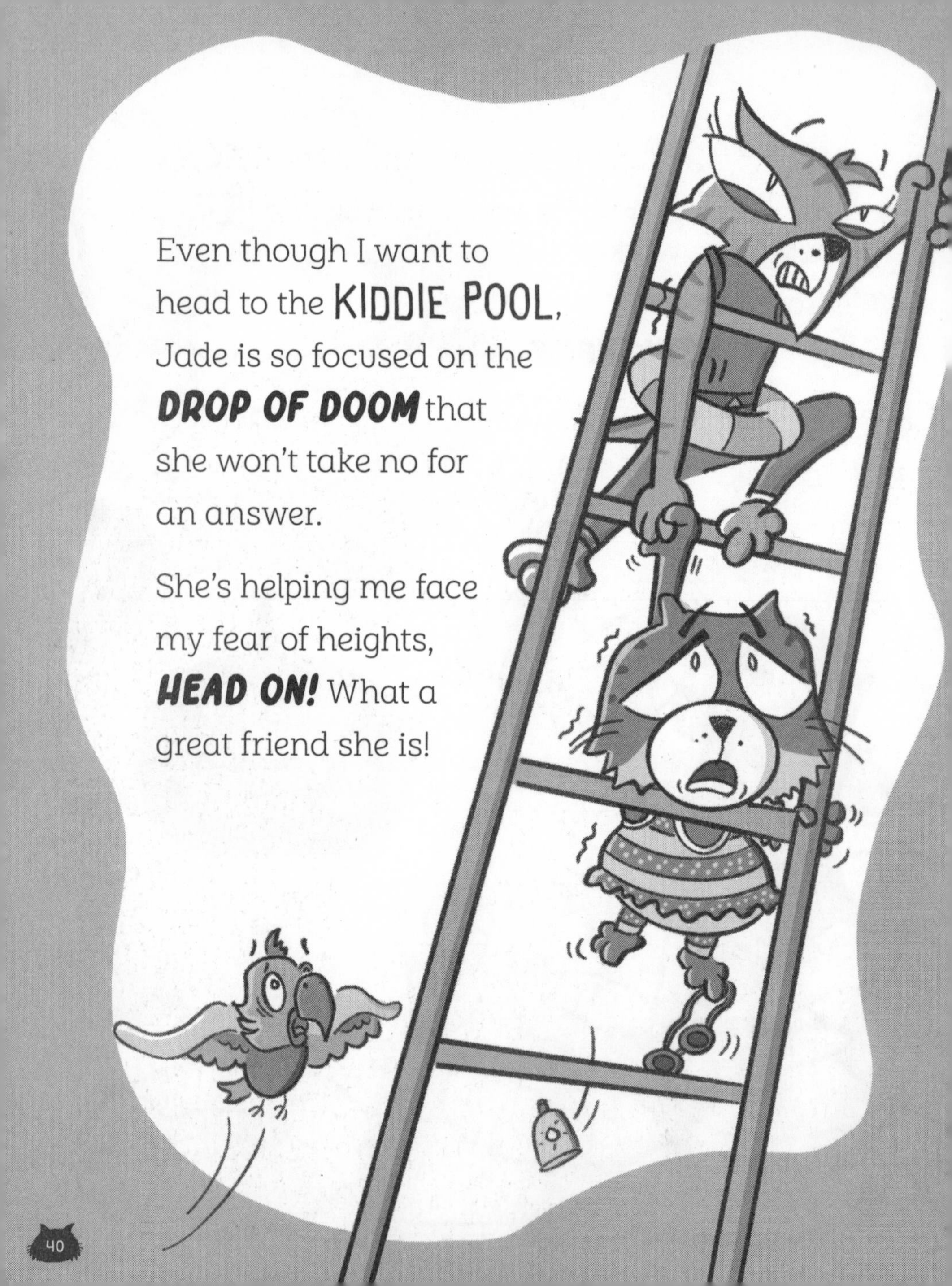

Even though I want to head to the **KIDDIE POOL**, Jade is so focused on the ***DROP OF DOOM*** that she won't take no for an answer.

She's helping me face my fear of heights, ***HEAD ON!*** What a great friend she is!

We find Furball at the very top of the **DROP OF DOOM** slide. He seems a little PUFFED.

'Kinda weird that the pool below is shaped like a **SKULL**,' says Jade.

'Maybe it's just your eyes playing tricks on you!' I reply, SHAKING too much to **THINK STRAIGHT**.

Besides, this day out is meant to be our **REWARD** from Ms Big Wig! I'm sure nothing bad is going to happen. And going on **SUPER HIGH** waterslides is supposed to be fun, right?

As I open one eye to peer over the edge, suddenly my head starts **SPINNING!**

'Guys, my tummy is a little upset,' I say.

'What smell?' I ask. 'I don't smell, do I?'

'Kit, why do you think you were **BANNED** from the local flower shop last week?'

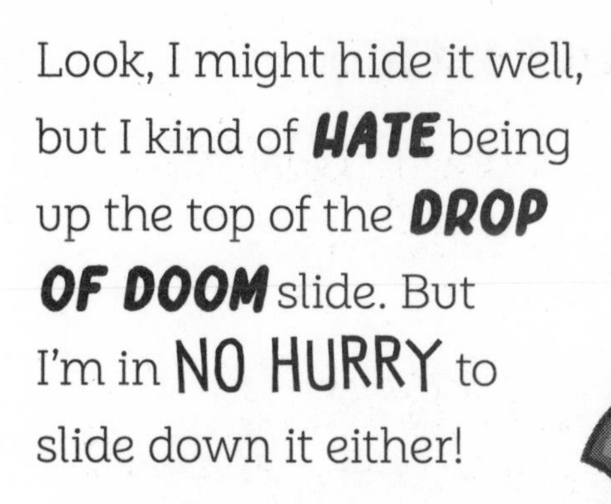

Look, I might hide it well, but I kind of **HATE** being up the top of the **DROP OF DOOM** slide. But I'm in NO HURRY to slide down it either!

I guess I'm a little nervous. And I talk a **LOT** when I'm nervous.

Do you like my goggles, Jade? How about my floaties? **COOL, HUH?**

Oh, I designed my swimsuit myself! **HEY!** Try on my new gadget watch, Jade. It's waterproof!

Jade?

JADE?

JAAAAAAADE?

I give Jade my **GADGET WATCH** to try on. This is a good excuse to hold her hand.

Jade keeps me steady. Even though I'm a proper **SPY** and still very, very **BRAVE!**

Then one of the park workers wakes Furball up by ***HELPING*** him on his way down the slide.

I notice my goggles moving. So I reach out to grab them, before I realise they're CAUGHT on Furball's tail. **UH-OH!**

He pulls me down the slide with him! But I'm still holding Jade's hand. **TIGHTLY!**

WHOOPS!

But, as I said, I am
VERY <u>VERY</u> BRAVE,
so I keep my cool as
we slide DOWN.

AAAAAAAUGH!

AND DOWN.
AAAAAAAAUGH!

AND DOWN

. . . even through

the dark bit.

Finally, we are all thrown up into the air,

Furball lands first.
BOMBS AWAY, PEOPLE!
SPLOOOSH!

Soon after Furball, Jade hits the pool as well. She does a **PERFECT** dive.

And I do a **PERFECT** dive too.

BELLY-WHACK!

'Well, that was, um, great!' I say. 'But **ONCE** is enough for me.'

But Jade does not reply. She is **GLARING** at the pool around us.

'Seems like there's less water in here than there should be,' says Jade.

'Well, Furball made quite a **SPLASH**,' I say.

Jade is right. Based on the **SILLY HEIGHT** we just dropped from, the pool should be DEEPER.

In fact, it feels like the water level is dropping by the second.

Then I get distracted by **BRIGHT COLOURS!**

As soon as we get there, Furball **BLASTS** me with the hose! He's **SUCH** a kidder!

But the water soon runs out.

At the same time, Jade **FLIPS** through the air to the very top of the water playground.

Jade looks out at the whole park.

'Kit, something doesn't SMELL right,' she calls.

'Sorry, might be my **BAD TUMMY** again.'

'Not just that . . . hmmm.'

'EVIL PLAN!'

cries Jade.

'Uh-oh,' I reply. 'That sounds even **WORSE** than WEEVIL JAM.'

5

'Looks like the park workers are pumping all the pool water into those **MASSIVE TANKS** out the back,' says Jade. 'Seems ***DODGY!***'

When Jade says something is DODGY, she's ALWAYS right. In fact, it's usually **DODGIER** than DODGEBALL!

'OH NO!' she cries. 'You won't believe who I just spotted!'

THE 'PURR-MINATOR?'

'Nope,' says Jade.

'Oh, is it your evil nan,

GRANDMA GASSY PANTS?' I ask.

SPIN SPIN SPIN!

I'm silent but **DEADLY!**

'No, not my Gran.'

'Is it . . . **FRANK?**' I ask.

'Wait, do you mean the CHEF from Furball's **FAVOURITE PIZZA SHOP?**'

'He always gets Furball's order wrong. Drives him **WILD!**'

'No, Kit. It's Furball's **OTHER** greatest enemy!'

'There's just SO many. Would it be easier if I looked for myself?'

'Much,' says Jade.

I build up the courage to climb to the TOP of the water playground and join her. 'Everything's so **LITTLE!**' I say.

'Hey, that's not a BADDIE! I thought you meant there was an **ENEMY** from **KLAWZ** wandering around,' I say, relieved. 'That's just the waterpark's owner, **WET WILLY!**'

'Are you **SURE** about that?' asks Jade. 'Check out the car.'

'Trembling tuna-cakes!' I reply. 'Is that Leadfoot's famous ***GAS-GUZZLER?***'

'Yep.'

'Then *that* means . . .'

'Sure does. Imagine Wet Willy **WITHOUT** his moustache and glasses!'

'Uh-oh, you're right!' I say. 'It's a disguise! That's Furball's ***GREATEST ENEMY!*** (Well, one of them). It's . . .'

Jade and I have just discovered that **LEADFOOT** - one of Furball's many 'Greatest Enemies' - is **HERE** at the waterpark!

Leadfoot has been pretending to be a regular business owner named **WET WILLY**. When in fact he is a **BIG BADDIE** from **KLAWZ**!

'Leadfoot **LOVES** hot rods! He's never shown interest in **POOLS** before. What's he up to?' I ask Jade.

'Perhaps he's recently got into **SYNCHRONISED SWIMMING**, like me?'

'Unlikely,' says Jade. 'No, Leadfoot must have an **EVIL PLAN**. We need to STOP him before it's too late! Where's Furball?'

'I should have known,' says Jade. 'Furball! Leadfoot is **HERE** at the waterpark!'

'What do I always say?' Furball replies. 'Let's save the spy business till ***AFTER*** I've eaten!'

'GUYS, COME ON! I've just ordered a **SPUCKET!**' says Furball.

'Is that **SPAGHETTI** in a **BUCKET?**' I ask. 'I've got to see this!'

My eyes wander to the SNACK BAR MENU!

'Personally, I'd like to try a ***SHARREL*** - a shake in a barrel.

But I also like the sound of a ***CHOOT*** - cheese in a boot.

Or maybe a ***KEBARROW*** - kebabs in a wheelbarrow!'

Jade's right. So, I borrow a nearby customer's tablet to **HACK** into the waterpark's computer network.

'Yep, Leadfoot has just about drained **ALL** the water from the park!'

Just then, a waiter interrupts, 'One **SPUCKET** for a Mr . . . Ball?'

'Whatever,' says the waiter.

'I hear CHOPPERS!' says Jade.

'Could be a coincidence,' I say, hoping for no more **COMPLICATIONS**. 'How do you know they're part of Leadfoot's plan?'

'Well, **YOU** tell **ME**,' Jade replies.

'Furball, Jade's right,' I say. 'As usual.'

♥ LEADFOOT
STACKS OF SNACKS
Oh, SPUCKET!
JUST SAY SPUCKET!
SAVOUR THE FISHY FLAVOUR

7

We creep closer and hide behind a water fountain. It's the perfect spot to **SPY** on Leadfoot and his gang.

I try to figure out Leadfoot's plan. Then, after QUITE SOME TIME, I say, 'I have **NO IDEA** what he's planning!'

'It **IS?**' I ask.

'Let's split up. We can still stop him,' says Jade as she cartwheels off.

'We **CAN?**' I call after her.

'Should've ordered my SPUCKET to go!' grumbles Furball.

'You **DIDN'T?**'

Then the water fountain STOPS.

We need a new hiding spot.

Suddenly, I feel my swimsuit tug on my neck. Then my feet lift
RIGHT OFF THE GROUND!
A helicopter grabs me by a HOOK and raises me into the AIR!
NOOOOOOOOOOOOO! I still have an UPSET TUMMY, you maniacs!

The chopper PLONKS me right back on top of the DROP OF DOOM platform again. And I think I might SPEW!
You really put the 'ILL' in VILLAIN!
DROP OF DOOM

I get distracted as Leadfoot's gang **SURROUNDS** Furball, below.

'We meet again, Furball, my old friend,' says Leadfoot.

'We're **NOT** friends, Leadfoot.'

Oh, no! I realise Furball and Leadfoot are locked in one of their classic **BAD JOKE** stand-offs. This could go on for hours!

Leadfoot, **WATER** fuss you've made here!
Well, first I bought a pool, then a waterslide. It's a **SLIPPERY SLOPE!**

The waterpark is quite the set up. You really must have **POOLED** your resources!
What will I do with you, now that you've found me out? I guess it **DEEP ENDS!**

Whatever you decide, Leadfoot, you'll find when it comes to swimming I'm RELAY fast!
Well, too bad you're surrounded, Furball. Like boiled water you'll be MIST!

'Furball, the **CHOPPERS!**' I cry from the very top of the suddenly windy slide, glad to have found something to distract him. 'They're **TAKING OFF!**'

Leadfoot's choppers are moving the MASSIVE WATER TANKS! But where are they carrying all that water? AND WHY?

The whole situation is **HOPELESS!** Worse than the time I invented ***SMOKED SALMON SMOKE BOMBS!***

'Trembling tuna-cakes, this is **BAD!**' I mutter to myself. 'What SPY GADGETS did I pack? Anything useful?'

I check my pockets and the first thing I find is a **MEOW-6** walkie-talkie.

SHUSH, NOW? How dare you? Is that you, umm, Nit?
Sorry, I wasn't talking to you! And my name's KIT, actually.
WHATEVER. So have you three stopped Leadfoot's evil plot?
No. We need help! Hang on, you KNEW Leadfoot was here? This day trip wasn't just a NICE REWARD?
Um ... oh dear, my phone is BREAKING UP.
You're on a WALKIE-TALKIE! Anyway, we need back up! Send every agent you have. How fast can you get here?
FIVE MINUTES! Four if I don't redo my lipstick! So let's say five.

Big Wig will be ***TOO SLOW!*** Especially now that Leadfoot's had Furball tied to the last remaining water tank.

'This waterpark is actually my **SECRET BASE!**' laughs Leadfoot. 'I've been sucking up water from the ocean and hiding it here for months!'

'Laugh all you want, Furball!' sneers Leadfoot. 'But if I don't get a **BAJILLION DOLLARS**, I'm gonna ***FLOOD THE CITY!***'

'Ha! Good one,' says Furball. 'Why would a petrol head like you want to **FLOOD** the city?'

'Well, sea levels will rise soon enough, anyway! So, I'll just switch to jet skis a little earlier, if I don't get my **MONEY!**'
The city is gonna be **WETTER THAN YOUR CHIN** at an all-you-can-eat buffet!

I watch in **PANIC** from the top of the Drop of Doom slide.

'Come on, Leadfoot. We both know Big Wig will ***never*** pay you,' cries Furball. 'She's **TIGHTER** than Kit's swimsuit!'

'Well, that's ***her*** choice!' laughs Leadfoot, as he jumps into the pilot seat of the last chopper. 'I just hope you all like **OCEAN VIEWS!**'

UH-OH. This tank's fuller than me after Christmas dinner!

CRAAAAACK!

CRAAAAACK!

The MASSIVE water tank is going to BURST!

I <u>HAVE</u> TO HELP FURBALL! The moment the tank blows he'll be swept away in a ***TIDAL WAVE!***

But I'm stuck at the top of the waterslide. The only way to get closer to him - and try to help - is to . . . ***GO DOWN THE SLIDE!*** Again.

'If only I'd brought my **BOOGIE BOARD**,' says Furball.

I lower myself to the entrance of the DROP OF DOOM slide. I see it's a **LOOOOOOOOONG** way down to the bottom. And there's barely enough water left in the pool . . .

But I ***HAVE*** to help save the city ***AND*** my best friend!

I close my EYES...
I cross my FINGERS...
I let out a little GAS...
Then I take a STEP onto the slide!

TREMBLING
TUNA CAKES!

But halfway down I **OPEN** my eyes.

I take a gadget from my pocket.

Now that I'm close enough to Furball, I **HURL** the gadget towards him.

I've heard cooler one-liners, but none that make **DENTAL HYGIENE** such a priority.

The toothbrush **SAILS THROUGH THE AIR**. For a moment I forget I'm even on the slide. My eyes dart from the toothbrush to Furball.

Furball watches the brush spinning towards him. But I'm staring at the cracks around him getting **BIGGER** and **BIGGER!**

ANY SECOND, THE TANK IS GOING TO BURST!

Furball's arms are **TIED!** He can't use them to catch the toothbrush!
But then I lose sight of the brush completely as water **EXPLODES** around him!
NOOOOOOOOO!

SPLOOOSH!!

9

I take cover at the base of the **DROP OF DOOM** slide as water ***SPEWS*** from the massive tank.

MORE AND MORE
AND MORE WATER
ROCKETS OUT!
It just keeps coming!
And just when I think it's over . . .
there's MORE!
I'll always remember you, Furball.
Return to sender, nude gerbil.

It seems to take **FOREVER** for the water to clear.

I take a deep breath, I think of my best friend, Furball, then - slowly - I look up at the **BURST TANK**.

And I see . . .

The **MAGNETIC TOOTHBRUSH** stuck to the broken tank and stopped Furball getting washed away. It SAVED him!

'See! This is why I always say **BRUSHING IS GOOD FOR YOU!'** I call.

But Furball doesn't reply. I'm sure he probably agrees.

Furball climbs down to the ground. **I RUN** to him. 'Bring it in, Big Guy!'

'I must admit, that was a handy **SPY GADGET**, Kit,' says Furball.

'Good one!' I laugh, but then I remember Leadfoot's **EVIL PLAN**. 'Furball, I know you probably have more hilarious TEETH JOKES to tell, but the city is in **TROUBLE!**'

'Huh?' I say, as Furball points up to the sky.

Jade has taken off in Leadfoot's **GAS-GUZZLER!** She's sped up a waterslide, jumping STRAIGHT for the nearest chopper!

HEY, THAT'S **MY** CAR! WHO DO YOU THINK YOU ARE?

10

Like a NINJA WARRIOR, Jade jumps from the **GAS-GUZZLER** to the landing skid of the closest chopper! Then she **swings** to the next two, like she's on monkey bars.

'She's going after Leadfoot!' I say. 'She has that ***WILD LOOK*** in her eye.'

'Like the look I get after eating curried scallop pies,' Furball agrees. 'They burn ***TWICE!***'

JADE SOMERSAULTS THROUGH THE AIR and grabs onto Leadfoot's chopper.

WHOOOOOOOSH
B.Y.O. SICK BAG! He-hee-hee!
TREMBLING TUNA-CAKES! Do you think she has some sort of plan?
You've MET Jade, right?

I **SQUINT** my eyes and notice Jade is still wearing my ***SPY GADGET WATCH!*** She whips it off and fastens it to Leadfoot's chopper!

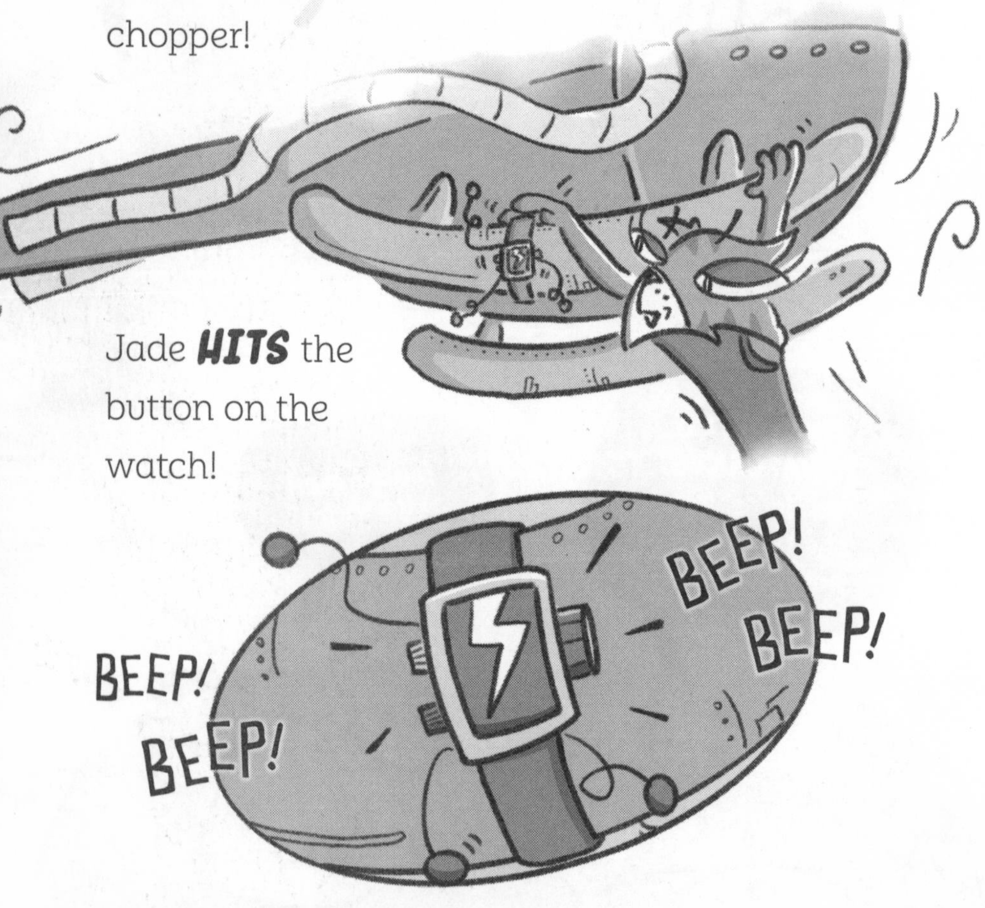

Jade ***HITS*** the button on the watch!

Then Jade **LETS GO** of the chopper!

ZOOMING down towards us, Jade **SPINS, TWISTS** and **SOMERSAULTS**.

Then she completes a perfect dive into the pool below.

'I taught her that,' says Furball.

But I'm not sure I believe him.

KAKABOOOOOOM
SUDDENLY,
THUNDER BOOMS
AND
LIGHTNING STRIKES
THE WATCH ON
LEADFOOT'S CHOPPER.

FZZZZT!
This is SHOCKING!
FZZZT!
FZZZZT!

Leadfoot's busted chopper FALLS from the sky.
Well, I guess WHAT GOES UP ...

So Leadfoot hits the chopper's ***EJECTOR BUTTON!***

11

Leadfoot pulls the parachute cord but he drops to the ground **FASTER** and **FASTER!** And – unlike Jade – he's **NOT** going to land in a pool.

'There **MUST** be another way,' says Furball.

'They're gadget undies, made of PARACHUTE MATERIAL. They'll break Leadfoot's fall!' I explain.

We **RUSH** to stretch them out.

Leadfoot lands -
in the undies!
WOOOMP!
But at SUCH SPEED he bounces
STRAIGHT BACK OUT!
Nice of you to DROP IN!
. . . into
Furball's
arms!

Unfortunately, the undies land on me. And I get a **BIT** stuck . . .

Just then, our **MEOW-6** boss, Ms Big Wig, finally arrives with back-up. She looks around and gives us a nod.

'Great job, Furball,' says Ms Big Wig, eyeing off Leadfoot who is now defeated. 'You truly are the **GREATEST SPY IN THE WORLD!**'

'I am?' mutters Furball.

'ACTUALLY, **YES! I AM!**'

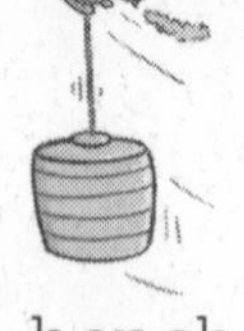
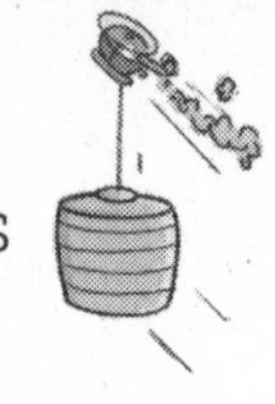

With their boss caught, Leadfoot's henchmen land their choppers under Jade's **WATCHFUL EYE!**

'You were AMAZING, Jade!' I cry as I shake off my undies.

'You too, Kit. I saw you **BRAVELY** go down the slide to save Furball. Nice.'

Even though I do ***NOT*** get a hug from Jade, I still have a ***SPRING*** in my ***STEP!*** Once again, I am proud to have helped put another evil member of **KLAWZ** behind bars!

'Big Wig, do you have the **MEOW-6** credit card handy?' Furball asks. 'Cos if you'd **REALLY** like to thank us.'

Food always tastes better when SOMEONE ELSE IS PAYING FOR IT!
JUST SAY SPUCKET!
SAVOUR THE FISHY FLAVOUR

SID FURBALL

WILL RETURN IN ...

BOOK TWO
FURBALL
TOP SPEED
COMING SOON!

ABOUT THE AUTHOR

ADRIAN BECK is an author from Melbourne who writes funny, action-packed stories for kids. As well as being a writer, Adrian is also definitely, definitely, DEFINITELY, not secretly a spy. And if he was a spy, it would need to be kept TOP SECRET . .. so, shhhhhh! Don't tell anybody! We need to trust you on this. Okay? Adrian's got a tough job writing books AND saving the world! Let's not blow his cover!

Along with the amazing *Furball* series, Adrian is the author of the *Derek Dool* series, the *Champion Charlies* series, the *Alien Zoo* series and co-author of the *Little Legends* series with Nicole Hayes, plus the *Kick it to Nick* series with AFL hall-of-famer Shane Crawford. Adrian has also written two picture books *Stop the Dad Jokes* (because he is a DAD-JOKER!) and *The Unfunny Bunny* (because he is a BUNNY! No, hang on, that can't be right).

Adrian has had a blast appearing at Sydney Writers' Festival, Melbourne's Kids' BookFest, Somerset Storyfest and many other literature festivals around Australia. He has also visited hundreds of schools to talk all about reading and writing and one day he hopes to visit YOUR school and meet YOU!

And lastly, he is DEFINITELY NOT a spy.

Promise.